ANDREW N

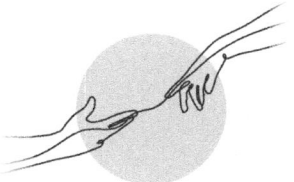

hey
you

Andrew Noelker
noelkerandrew@gmail.com

Copyright © 2023

All rights reserved. No part of this book may be reproduced, stored in a retrieval system, or transmitted in any form or by any means, electronic, mechanical, photocopying, recording, scanning, or otherwise, without the prior written consent of the author.

life is worth living if you have something to live for
for my family, specifically my parents
this is for you

Table of Contents

introduction	7
1 in 8 billion	8
roses are red	10
get you back	13
hamilton	14
hope in the fight	16
fairytale	19
how many more?	20
need you here	23
moon knows	24
unique	27
pulchritude	28
preview	30
then I can die	33
modern love mystery	34
her hair	37
may 1st	38
hey you... pt. 1 (voicemail)	41
stoplight	42
pink parasol daffodil	45
carousel	46
NoNeed2	49
no matter what	50
opposites of love	53
how come?	54
necessary	57
sunburn	59
profound	60
rewind	62
something for something	65
for my son pt. 1	66
you should see	68

keep going	71
alyssastockkk	72
the man I'll be next week	75
over the rainbow	76
hey you... (voicemail) pt.2	79
thank you God	80
what if?	82
I have a question	85
love... no, moving out	86
until I'm dead	89
lie for love	90
the bar, where love lives	92
smile	95
wipe it all away	97
something real	98
try to stop	101
special day	102
lucky	104
window shutters	106
my favorite introduction	108
sometimes	111
1000	112
advantageous	115
ebullience	116
addiction	118
from giving flowers to swiping right	120
hours	123
send me to hell	124
acknowledgements	126
for my readers	127
about the author	129

hey you

introduction

this book started as a suicide note.

well...

not entirely, but that's how I started writing. I wrote for 30 days straight, depressed, in the bathroom of my college house until the note disappeared one night.

it was a sign.
a sign to get up, get help, and start pursuing my newfound passion.
a sign to find people who value thoughts, feelings, and emotions.
a sign, that if I want to better this world, I have to show others that peace and love truly exists.

that's what I hope to accomplish with this first collection of poems. I have found comfort in words that rhyme. I hope these poems fill your heart with joy for love, give closure to those holding on in heartbreak, and show the hopelessness that there is hope when the light goes out.

while in rehab, one of the nurses greeted me with a "hey you" each morning. it was a nice start to the day and gave me the fortitude to keep going. those "hey you's" showed me there's always someone looking out for you even when it doesn't feel like it. this book is my "hey you" to you. you guys are my world.

I'm glad I found you.
yes, YOU.

hey you,
thanks for being here.

1 in 8 billion

1 in 8 billion
In it's truest form - my first poem ever written
Every day, questioning why life is worth living.
Why it's easier taking instead of giving.
Why there's less light than there is dark.
Every day, searching, in need of a spark.
Wishing to never awake from our slumbers.
(sigh)
Our answer for the purpose of life lies within the numbers.
All it takes is 1 random person to prove,
the meaning behind the 8-letter phrase,
"I Love You."
Stay strong, love.

roses are red

roses are red
violets are blue
life was so much easier
when I was with you

you used to love cute poems
that started like that
they were your favorite
randomly sending them in our chat

do you still like those cute poems
now that I'm not in the picture?
because whenever I see one now
it's an instant mood killer

those poems remind me of you
and bring about thoughts of everything I should've done
to keep you around and
have the forever honor to call you my one

I should've prayed more for you
and worked to get a little stronger
I should've shared my deepest secrets
like how badly I want to raise a daughter
and be the best father
I should've told you how much I love you
instead of saving to share them at the altar
I should've
I should've kissed you longer

do you send cute poems to someone new?
send him this one, if you do

roses are red
and violets are blue
give her the world
because she's way more than just a pretty view

Andrew Noelker   **hey you**

get you back

it's been a year, since you left
I still can't get you out of my head

I wake up to the thought of you and your beauty
I spend my whole day reminiscing, truly
then go to bed, planning how I'll fix it,
so we can love more smoothly

I think I've figured it out,
(how to get you back)
I have everything I need
everything except...
a time machine.

hamilton

I live in a small town with big hopes
a town that the Great Miami River splits in half
where happiness derives
and pretty smiles on people that love to laugh

where a railroad creates unwanted traffic
a town that enjoys launching pumpkins and slicing ice
where sculptures come to life
and loving teachers give great advice

three bridges that connect the east to the west
river dams with flowing sides
good food surrounded by good company
in mom-and-pops like *Flub's*, *Jolly's*, ever-growing *Hyde's*

a town swelled with vacant factories that propagate silence
and a statue of Alexander greeting every guest with a wave
where artists settle to find inspiration
a town with endless memories for the names on each grave

a town filled with love
from truck beds at the *Holiday Drive-In Theatre*
every pour from behind bar counters
in each sip of bourbon or beer
there's nowhere I'd rather be than here

I've found this town's coffee often fixes my mind
and comfort to write my thoughts behind the *True West* sign
I've found devotion is common
from the townspeople and even the animals that roam
because everyone here, knows
Hamilton is home

hope in the fight

my therapist told me something yesterday
that completely changed the way I think

"You can't defeat darkness by running from it."

I responded,

*"I always thought I could outrun it.
I'm pretty good at escaping.
instead, you want me to stay put
and face it head on, that's what you're saying?"*

after a little explaining
with some words that felt draining
she was right, it was my mindset that needed changing

trust me, I know it's hard
thinking running from your problems is smart
guarding your heart
waiting for the foundation to crumble
forcing you to restart

please know, you're not alone
that it's okay to show, the things you try to hide
because when it's dark, and you feel lost in the night
there is always hope.

there is a light.

so when you can't decide to either run or fight
just know, embracing the darkness doesn't make you heartless
not quite
no matter how hard it's been the darkness will never win

don't run or hide,

you are the light.

I believe in you, stop running, and go fight

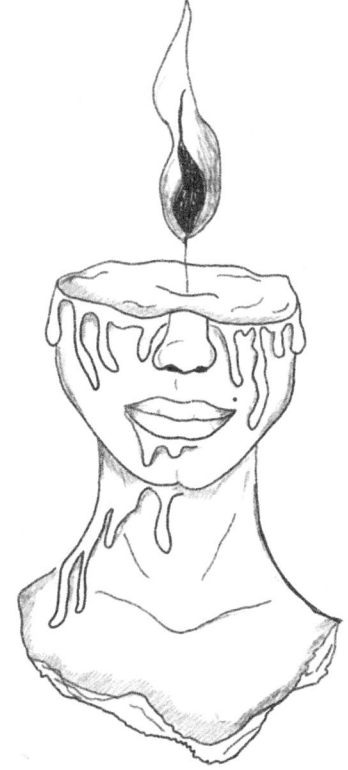

by Lizzie Kolde

fairytale

falling in love is usually a surprise, right?
at least I think it should be

that's why I'm having trouble saying hi to you
I want our first meeting to be
like it is in the movies
when the guy helps pick up the girl's scattered things on the floor
or the soldier meeting a local when off at war
what about running into the girl for the first time since you kissed
on the playground at the age of four?

what a dream
I think that's what we all want, right?
spontaneous love that's so exciting, it's like flying our first kite

it wouldn't be very natural if I planned to run into you on purpose
plus, I'd be nervous
so instead, I'm going to keep going about my day
chasing happiness, knowledge, and laughter
until the day we cross paths, the fairytale meeting we deserve,
and live happily ever after

how many more?

the bathroom floor was pleasantly cold
as I laid there, my head pounding, but numb
and violently shaking the energy out my leg
on beat, like a drum

you do a lot of thinking during panic attacks

i was scared to move my body
so i laid as still as a statue
somehow, I still couldn't catch my breath
like I had just run a mile or two

get out of your head

stomach bloated and my mind overheating
"has the sun exploded?"
"is my brain bleeding?"
irrational thoughts noted
"is it the panic attack
or the side effects from having covid?"

you're going crazy...

I've had hundreds of panic attacks but this one broke me.
monday. january 14th, 2022.
although I've moved on, I will never forget.

in that moment, I feared death.
and after, I feared living.
until I learned that, neither is worth fearing at all.

how many more panic attacks do you have planned for me God?
your plan is to make me stronger

if are you preparing me for a larger war
i'm ready
because to put it frankly, God
i'm not scared anymore

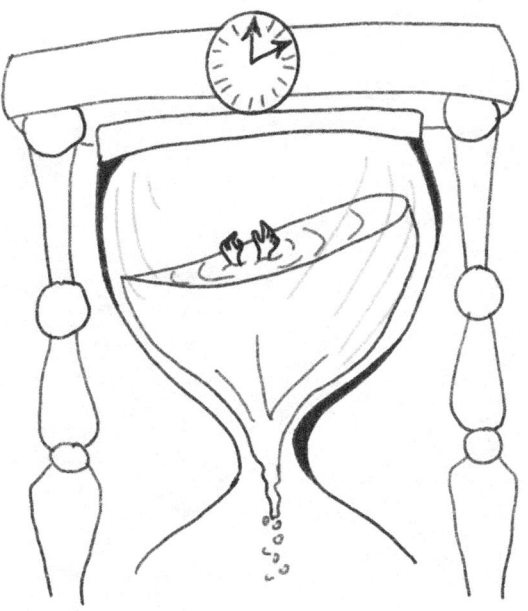

by Lizzie Kolde

need you here

you look great today
I'm not just saying that because you are important to me
I genuinely mean it

I'd say it every day but after some time
you stop believing
insecurities start increasing
your eyes deceiving

I wish you could see what I see
just like the Grand Canyon or looking out the window of a plane
this view never gets old
and I'm never going to stop telling you
until you're sold

you deserve the world

and the world I live in wouldn't be complete without you in it
My Times Mag Women of the Year
so, promise me, you will start saying happy things
when you look in the mirror?
and if you can't, I'll keep saying it until it's clear
because...

I need you here

moon knows

I asked the moon about you
I hope that's alright
because I figured he knew
since he sees you every night

it's funny
when I told him your name
his face was glowing
and more than usual
his happiness, too much to contain,
a feeling that hits close to home
the same feeling I feel in my brain

he likes you too
in fact,
he told me
the equivalent of the North Star
in the sky to us
would be you, on earth, to him

he said he gets to see your smile a lot
apparently, you like the night
more than the light
which I guess would make sense
because why would something as bright
as you
want to be noticed?

so now, me and the moon are friends
because we share something in common

oh that reminds me of something I've forgotten

he wanted me to tell you
"thank you"
for illuminating the night
when he runs out of light

he couldn't have said it any better
because as I lay here in the bed of my truck
tonight
I realized without you
I would have nothing to write

unique

if I were to ask you for your number, would you give it to me?
I know, I'm a little shy & not the best looking guy
but I think I offer something different
from the other men you might see
something unique

like hungry hyenas hovering over their prey
I'm not the only one that wants to call you "home"
I'm sure you already know

unlike the others though,
I'm not going to use you
or treat you like trash
I want all of you

to hold you when your days suck
show you off, show the guys what happens
when you shoot your shot,
and end the night telling you how gorgeous you are,

you know, in case you forgot

I want the good and the bad
unlike the rest
I don't need your best, or to get you undressed
I want you for you
and the love that's true

I just want you as my own
So, can I put you in my phone?

pulchritude

(n.) - physical beauty; comliness

imagine if pulchritude was put on the back burner
when growing a genuine connection
leading to more authentic affection, less hurtful rejection,
and better humane direction

but there's no rose without a thorn
no light without a shadow

so, if you're reading this, go out and spread love to everyone
attractive or not
good things will come back to you in return,
your dream person too
so give it all you have got
one day you'll look back and wonder why you
deserve such a good life and you'll say

"jackpot"

do unto others... well, you know the rest

preview

I don't know when I'll start loving again
but I do know that when the time comes
I'll be ready

I wonder
if it's you
reading this right now

and if it is,
there's a few things about me that I want to tell you
as a little preview

I love hard
spring is my fav season because of how the flowers smell
when I ride with the windows down

I like to play hide and seek with my dog,
yes, the game
where you hide in closets and under beds,
he's my best friend

I have a tender heart and fragile mind
so I write to escape and put my thoughts on paper
instead of letting them wander around in my head

I don't enjoy controversy but will fight for what's right,
a passive enforcer
and sometimes I struggle loving myself
because that type of love is hard

but if it is you, I can promise you
I won't need a reason to love you in any season
I'll find myself spending more time with you instead of my dog
& never wanting to escape your presence
we'll rarely fight, & if we do, we'll always make things right

and I'll love you so hard,
convincing you to love yourself will be easy.

hope to see you soon,
you know, if it is you.

then I can die

I don't care about you getting me gifts on my birthday
and I don't want anything on my valentine's or christmas
because after a few weeks
the happiness tied to the gift goes away

every one's love language is different
don't get me wrong, I enjoy giving
so, if you want to be spoiled, I can do that
but I find love in living

like seeing your reaction when you try something new
how the sun rays feel as they slice through our joint hands
when we travel together in good weather
to beaches with pretty sand
or helping our kids set up & plan their first lemonade stand

whatever it is, together and living
as long as you are by my side
and we can say

"there's nothing left we haven't tried."

then I can die, a happy guy

modern love mystery

there will come a time
when wearing no makeup
isn't a crime

when relationships harness more love than hate
when it's normal to bring flowers to the first date

when the jitters around them go away
and you feel at home
but homesick
when you realize you can't stay

I want to get back to the good ole days
the "hey she has a crush on you." phase
and relationships didn't feel like a maze

I want love
the when life gets tough
and the road gets rough
"we'll get through it" stuff

I'm a nice guy
that's how I was raised to be
my way of flirting isn't being mean

conflicts aren't made a scene
all because I care
it is our hearts we'll share

so, let's ditch history
so, we can get past
the modern love mystery
that nice guys finish last

by Lizzie Kolde

her hair

it swings in the wind
which provokes an elegant song
in my head that I
can't fully describe
kind of like how a wind chime moves
in the breeze and sings its little melody

that type of vibe

a melody that will turn into a memory
by time or by distance
either a fallout or the full length of our existence

but I really do hope it is the latter

her hair
this melody

is my destiny

may 1st

today, I caught myself smiling...
and I think it's because of

beautiful fluidity, the wind shaking the trees
buzzing, the gnawing of wood from the worker bees
usually, I can wait a few weeks before the heat starts
burning the tips of my knees
it's only the first of May

you know, I love the spring
because it reminds me of you

how your hair swings in the wind, just as the trees do
every room you enter
buzzing, flocking to you,
the queen, encircling you in the center
and how you make me better

I'm so lucky, honestly
you make me think constantly
how much longer I can wait before I can make you mine forever
for the day, I get down on a burnt knee
and live in love as beautiful as a day in the spring
that, I can guarantee

after my eyes open and before they close, I will pray
that my future includes you, every year and all the days
before and after the first of May

by Lizzie Kolde

by Jalon Smith

hey you... pt. 1 (voicemail)

Hey...you

if I had to choose between

starting my life over from the beginning
without the knowledge I have gained

or

getting the opportunity to plan the rest of my life,
exactly how I want, all the way to the very end

I'd have trouble deciding

part of me wants to encounter meeting you,
the love of my life for the first time, again

but

the other part of me would love to be able
to spend the rest of my life with you

but if I had to decide, I think I know my answer

instead of forcing you to be in my future,
i'd relive the moment I knew you were my one
because the love I have now, is more than enough
a godsend
& hope we'd make it to the very end

stoplight

I had a dream about you last night
again
well, it was more about us but
it made me think why the possibility of us
is only practical when my eyes are shut

it was a quick dream
you looked like an angel
how you usually do but shining a little brighter
I was stopped at a red light, and I looked over
to see you were in the car next to me
we locked eyes, then the light turned green
but we stayed there, afraid to lose each other
a spell we were under
and so serene, we both felt seen
then I woke up

I wonder if you dream about me too
or you secretly think that I'm cute, and I don't even know it
and those teasing comments you make is how you show it
now I don't want to blow it but I gotta say something soon
because I need to find out

like stop lights, red and green
sometimes the same love is said
and sometimes it's not meant to be
I gotta figure out if you belong in my head
and if it was smart to stay put when the light
turned green

I'm gonna ask, the next time I see you
hopefully, I get the answer I need
because I'd much rather spend time
with you in person,
instead of just in my dream

by Rosie Fernandez

Andrew Noelker **hey you**

pink parasol daffodil

I'm sorry, ladies
for all the boys
who use you
like kids do with their toys

our world is a museum
and women are the art
I'm doing my part
in changing the culture
boys, if you're not in her heart
keep the hands off the sculpture

a pink parasol daffodil
it's my favorite flower
white petals, pink bud on the top
like a penthouse in a tower

this flower and a woman are similar

the white pedals as the woman's body
the pink as her heart and head
her essence and soul matter more
so, stop trying to get in her bed

this world will be such a better place when
boys decide sooner
that they would rather be men

carousel

18 years ago, I used to love going to the zoo
because I knew
I was going to ride the carousel
my favorite ride since I turned two

I'd race to find my favorite horse
where happiness is stored, the source
the silver one, no scratches
with white and black patches

many years have passed but nothing's really changed
instead of a carousel, it's life
and instead of horses, I'm racing to find my wife

the girl who I've waited all this time for
the one that takes my breath away
who makes my world go round

racing to find the girl who supplies all my joy
just like the carousel did, when I was just a boy
from amusement park rides to finding the girl I'll always love
a ride I'll never want to get off of

NoNeed2

she's you
the girl I'm meant to spend the rest of my life with
the girl who runs out of the church next to me
after saying I do
she's you

I know, it sounds crazy
I've spent all of this time searching,
my heart burning and, in my bed, turning,
yearning for the perfect woman to come along

I even asked God awhile back
to show me a sign
when the girl enters my life
the ONE I get to call my wife

my sign came yesterday
in a "NoNeed2" license plate
of course... I hate
how shrewd He can be

I've seen your name three times today
which can't be a coincidence
all this searching for brilliance
you've been here all along
my girl of significance

now I'm positive that
you are the 1
because if he knew
she's you
then it has to be true

no matter what

I hate it when you talk about yourself like that
trust me, I totally understand how you feel
when it seems like every day is a fight
and the expectations from others deem to be real

but please, you have to stop, you are so much more
nowhere near a mistake,
someone no one can hate,
you are beautiful, kind, and the love you show others
is hard to ignore
not worthless nor should you feel guilty
there's so much you still have to live for

you're, a blessing to me and everyone around you
no
no
no
if, and, or buts

I'm going to keep reminding you that
I'll always be here, every day, no matter what

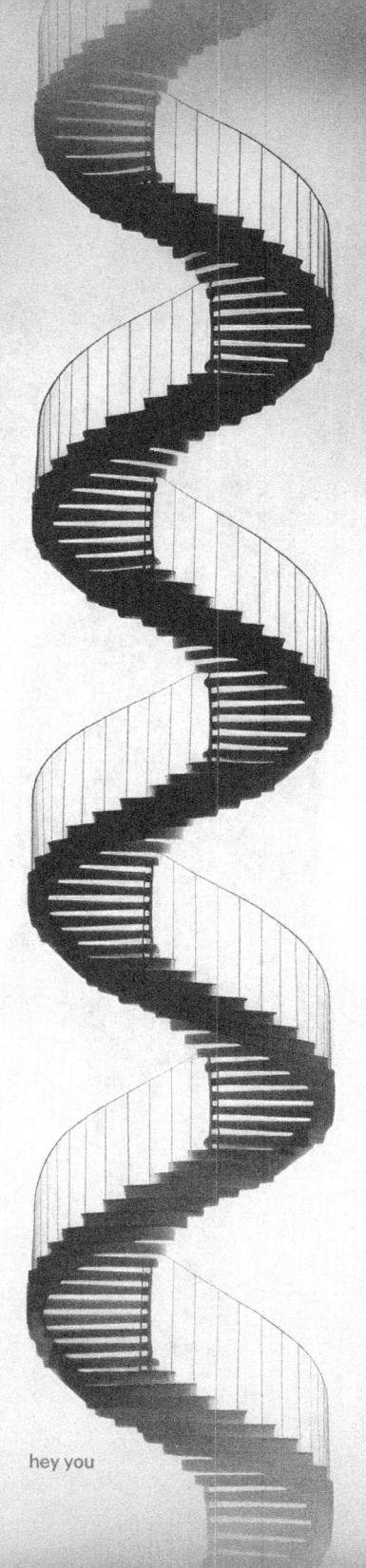

52 Andrew Noelker   **hey you**

opposites of love

it'll always be me and you
I will never say
I don't think it's us
our love is perfect
and it's not true that
you aren't my soulmate
I repeat it over and over in my head
I don't deserve you
I got to give credit where credit's due
sometimes I think I'm crazy
but I won't ever tell you
we aren't meant for each other

now read it up from bottom to top.

how come?

I get it
it's hard to see it any different
if you've experienced anxiety, please stick around
I promise you
this will pique your interest

when the dark clouds turn to rain
and rain begins the flood
or you get a cut
and out comes the stream of blood

this is what you overlook...
the flood encouraged the flower bud
the gold uncovered from the mud
the scab buried the wound from the fall or thud

during an anxiety attack,
it's easy to notice
your heart racing like a train
pins and needles, piercing the skin like rain
a volcano ready to erupt in the brain
feeling stuck, tied to the bottom of the ocean by a chain

anxiety isn't all bad
if you didn't have it
your love for others wouldn't be a habit

you understand
because you know
what it feels like when life feels low

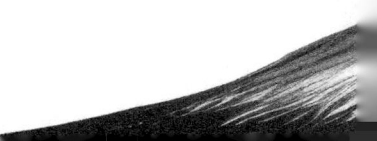

you're a leader
careful consideration,
can't function without some
because you see
every outcome

how come?
you think it's bad?

every attack or anxiety occasion
you can use for motivation
anxiety is perceived as a warning but
it's really
a superpower that you're ignoring

necessary

there are two ways people look for love,
I suppose
one is the dire need to find a new love
when your last leaves you bored
the other... well, is to spread love even if you're ignored
until God places your person right in front of you,
the person that will give you that love back
until you're restored

you see,
one is permanent and the other is temporary
but no matter the circumstance, in the end
we find that love is necessary

whatever it is
whatever you are looking for
I hope that it's everything you want
and that they never want to leave you and go out the door
I really hope so
so that you don't have to go searching anymore.

Andrew Noelker **hey you**

sunburn

07/25/23

I got a sunburn yesterday
and when I went out to cut my grass today
I realized something

it probably wasn't smart to expose my burns to more sun

just like it's probably not smart
to expose yourself to the person that has already
hurt you once before

profound

there's just something about you
that I can't wrap my finger around

like a puzzle in need of its last piece
I can't figure it out
could it be those green eyes
that prove you tell no lies

or is it the way
your hair falls beautifully off the sides of your face
stunning like fresh flowers in a vase

it's on the tip of my tongue
the trait of yours that makes me feel young
like the lullabies we sung

I can hear them now

that's what it is
the thing about you that makes you so profound
so calmly,
it is how your words leak from your mouth
onto the ground

your voice is my favorite sound

rewind

I was wrong
awhile back we were parked on a hill that overlooked the city
& staring out the sunroof of my car at the stars,
we counted sixty
I looked over to you as you were still gazing, how did I snatch a girl this pretty?
this is mine
I stretched my hand, to rest on your thigh
then you look over and we locked eyes

"could I ask you a question?", you said.
                                                    "of course," I replied.

you asked me, "imagine you could rewind the clock &
go back to one day in your life to live one single moment again,
what would it be?"

I know I said something stupid,
like sitting on the beach-drinking tea
or the time I hit 2 home runs in Tennessee
something so stupid, I guarantee, she wouldn't even remember

I think about that night a lot
because it was one of my favorite memories with you
and if you asked me, today, if I could go back to live a single
moment again
I'd pick that night
when we were still learning to love
when we were staring at the stars that were unusually bright
when I was staring in the eyes of my future bride
and before our love together, died.

so, looking back, I was wrong
maybe if I had said something different, something sweet
to show you I have a tender heart that loves with all its might
then maybe I wouldn't be sitting here wishing you'd come back
so, I could make things right

something for something

when we plan to hangout,
what feeling do you look forward to the most?

would it be feeling the heat, while in my arms
as it radiates off my tender heart?

or, to finally feel accepted and complete?
Which is all you've ever wanted from the very start.

all I want is to get the opportunity to unveil love
like you've never seen before
and get to call you mine forever,
like a painting on the wall,
my beautiful work of art

soulmates or love companions
I will give you my all and never let you feel alone
because I know what it feels like to be abandoned
unacceptable for us people that are grown

in the end, I want you to know
I will give you genuine love in exchange for devotion

quid pro quo

for my son pt. 1

my notes app is filled with things I don't want to forget
one of those notes is labeled "for my son"
a list of things I want to relive with him
well, if I were to have one

but since he's not here yet, I thought I'd share them with you
and show you my excitement for when I get the chance to
but just a few

I can't wait to see his face when he touches grass for the first time
or the time I need to catch him when he finds some stairs to climb

I can't wait to tell him that girls have cooties
then he finds one to love, that he'll say is "a thing of beauty"

I can't wait to show him how to love with the way I love his mom
and to see it in action during things like his homecoming or prom

I'm so excited
not kidding, I have a whole list,
these were just a few
if I were to share more,

it would need a pt. 2

you should see

what do you see in me that keeps you around?
is it how I look, how I act, or how I sound?
what makes me special? because I'm confused
why a messed-up boy with a heart that's just a little bruised,
piques the interest of a perfect person like you?

I may not be what you want
there's more to me than what you see
I don't want to fool you, so let me give you a little behind the scenes

you should see the clutter and disorder in my room
or hear me sing, I'm never in tune
you should see my clothes in my closet, no sign of fashion
or the lack of muscle for my bodies daily action, an accident waiting to happen

you should see how long it takes for me to get ready
and how I'm always nervous
so, I feel bad to take pictures for people because I can never keep it steady

you should see me embarrass whoever is with me
because of all my antics
or if I was stuck in a elevator with a group of people,
I'd be the one who panics

I'm just a boy from Ohio
I'm nowhere near extraordinary
other than leading with peace, unfortunately
I'm nothing out of the ordinary

there are guys out there who have the whole package
what I know I have
are values that are important to me

compassion
love, generosity, service, affection
heart, empathy, purpose
and the skill of listening and paying attention

although some of my attributes might not be tangible
I'm proud to see my qualities grow tall and wide,
like when a spark meets something flammable

what I have I am proud of
especially that I have you,
and your love that I have found
the person who sees all the imperfections
of a messed-up boy from Ohio
and decides to stick around

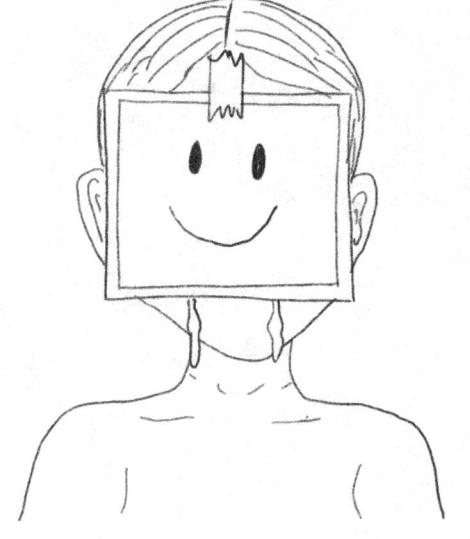

by Lizzie Kolde

keep going

you are important
your life might seem like a maze right now
or you feel like every day you are getting knocked down
but now is not the time to quit
you've come so far and have so much left to see
and if the people around you haven't told you yet,
you can take it from me

good things are coming for you, that, I can guarantee

so, if today, all you managed to do was get out of bed
I am proud of you
and if tomorrow, you can't get out of your head
I'm always one phone call away

today's struggle is tomorrow's spirit
keep going

alyssastockkk

there's this girl
that I found on TikTok
her story has changed my life
she goes by the name @alyssastockkk

been through a lot
health problems, physically
bouts with the brain, mentally

she's the epitome of strength
through it all she lives her life, fearlessly
has fun but still takes life, seriously
and in the process
has become a superhero, coincidentally

batman, the hulk, or superman
none of them can compare
pain is normal for her now
and she's still as lively as Times Square

you know...
if I had a penny for every time a guy has told me
"women are stronger than men"
my wallet would be empty
and I'd be so broke

which is a shame
because the longer I live and the more I see
I don't need a guy to tell me

it's time to clear the room of smoke
the strength of a woman
is no joke

the man I'll be next week

he'll get back to lifting
and eating the right way
start loving himself
despite what people say

he'll get back to church
and thanking God
writing his thoughts every day
even if they're a little odd

his hair will dry nicely
but won't care if it fails to
he'll feel all emotions
contrary of what other males do

he'll wear those pants
the ones they said looked stupid
and take his shirt off to cut the grass
because skinny doesn't matter when it's humid

he will love
more than his heart may allow
and be much happier
just 7 days from now

I'll do everything I've been saying I need to do
a new man in awe and unable to speak
I'm proud,
proud of the man I'll be next week

over the rainbow

somewhere over the rainbow
mythical, and way up high
there's a world that people dream of
invisible to the naked eye

a land packed with laughs and smiles
perfect breeding ground for devotion and felicity
a land many outcasts yearn
with bleating sounds for emotion and simplicity

where guys still open the passenger door
and dancing in the rain is a normal incidence
where every love story is one you'd read in a romance novel
and "kissing" photo booth images are limitless

there's a flight heading out next week
it seems I have an extra ticket
would you like to join me?
say yes, you'll be proud you did it

wait a minute...
this mythical world
we already live in it

so, turns out we won't have to visit
but that life I described
if that's the life you aren't living
I can give you
that of what you are missing

78 Andrew Noelker **hey you**

hey you... (voicemail) pt.2

hey you...
it's me again

I just wanted to let you know
there's no need to rush
life is better when you take it slow

it's okay to take a break
breathe
let's do it together

1
2
3

(breath)

good things are coming for you, I know it
you are

strong,
fearless,
determined

so, go show it

thank you God

I have to tell you about this girl I ran into yesterday
I was down at the park walking my dog
a dark cloud emerged from over the tree line
we weren't gonna make it to the car in time

I heard some heavy footsteps behind me
it was her
a bright smile, heavy breathing,
this is a weird way of meeting, under this canopy
I thought

she was immaculate, perfect, unflawed
her blue eyes matched the blue in the skies
from five minutes prior
so lively, she lit a fire
within my heart, that I couldn't get to start

and as she knelt next to my dog being gentle
from his eyes
I could tell even he knew she was special

I didn't think I'd find love, under a tree
But I guess what they say is right
"wonders will never cease"

we exchanged numbers
and as the rain began to stop
I looked up to see something so odd
there was only one dark cloud in a barren blue sky
"thank you God."

what if?

I met the love of my life today
well, I haven't met you yet but,
I said "hey",
as you passed me sitting at my gate in terminal A

unfortunately, you were heading the other way.

stunned, you left me shocked
eyes locked, time froze as everyone walked
then the butterflies flocked

you made my heart stop
thin top, little glasses
jeans with colorful patches
everything, on you matches

what if? what if it was?
man, it could've been us
but you're too good for me
silly for me to think that we could even be

you're probably leaving for New York
or maybe you're going down to San Antonio
I know we'd be a ways apart
but distance is just a test of how far love can go

wherever you end up
I hope you find the man of your dreams
someone who makes you feel seen
treats you like a queen
someone who craves you like caffeine

as he should, and if you don't
I know someone who would

sincerely,
the guy who said "hey" from terminal A

I have a question

might be jumping the gun, can't lie
and I may be reaching with this one, but I
really think we have something remarkable,
rare, unbeaten by every obstacle, others say
"yeah, that's true love. it really is possible."

make me the happiest man in the world
and say yes to this question
every first letter from each line, all seven
?

love... no, moving out

when I was a kid
I dreamt of the day
when we would have our first kid
                               no, when I find my own place

is $700 a month a lot?
I don't even know if I have that much
September, we'll tie the knot
                   no, this apartment doesn't need a woman's touch

I'm thinking I'll paint it green
or maybe it should be blue
gonna need two pillows
one for me and one for...

no

tomorrow I wake up in my own apartment
that comes with a view
but my view
used to be you

it was always going to be us, through and through
"you're crazy" you would say to learn how much time I've spent
wishing you'd come back to live in my heart
and pay no rent

I wish it was still salvageable
because you were heaven sent
that life was fun without a doubt
maybe I should focus more on love...
                                       no, moving out

until I'm dead

you make me feel... alive
I mean, that's the best way I can explain it... alive

kind of like how you feel when the windows are down
during a late drive
on a cold, Midwest, January night
or kind of like how you feel on the first day of vacation

when road or sky
turns to hot sand, that's - oh so white
it's kind of like how you feel... taking a test unprepared
with no confidence in sight
then finding out, you went 25/25, all answers right

I've never felt this way about a person until I met you
you're all I can think about, when I'm out or in bed
so please, stay
I want to feel alive, until I'm dead

lie for love

I went on my second date last week
& she asked me about the girls in my past
I had no idea what to say
"I didn't think I'd get this question today"
but I'll answer it anyway

the little workers in my mind,
scrambled through all the cabinet files trying to find
how we were going to get out of this one
but they ended up excuseless, none

my mind went numb
then the memories of us started to flood

it'd be wrong to tell her that you were my everything
it'd be wrong to say you were "all I ever want and need"
it'd be wrong to tell her that you were so right for me
how your hugs felt like home
how your subtle voice sent goosebumps through skin to the bone

for as much as I want to tell her about you
I just can't

I can't tell her that
I keep my room clean because you used to
or that I fix her hair behind her ear because you liked that
or how I'm afraid to ask her what she wants to eat?
because that question made you mad

to be honest, I'd feel bad
and you know I don't like lying
but in this case, it's either that or fall asleep crying

what's the point in trying
I can't tell her that I thought it should've been me and you forever
so, I guess I'll lie
and hope that she can do you better

the bar, where love lives

I notice the hair on the back of my neck stand up
usually when someone's watching me
I don't know why but most of the time I'm right about it too
in this bar, where silence has disappeared, and the mood is blue
I'm on this barstool and I can feel the vibration of the music
through the wood
I don't know why I'm here, but my vision's so clear
except I'm dizzy, I'm ditzy, I'm spinning
I don't know how many I've had, but it's probably too much
cold to the touch but every beer makes me feel a little warmer
inside

smiles surround me except on the faces
of the 20-year-olds outside whose fakes got
denied
I feel my shoes slide
but the floor's syrupy, and it's sticking
and the music drowns out every slippery thought
I don't know how many I've had, but it's probably too much
I fought my way up out of my seat
and I notice the hair on the back of my neck stand up
I'm usually right about it too

then I turn around
the most gorgeous woman I have ever seen before me
her silky-smooth hair, teeth so neat they don't even look real
I catch her pupils dilate, as my reflection appears, like they do in mirrors
we go on to talk for hours
and by the end, we both knew, this was love
I don't know how many I had, but I think it was just enough
anymore, I wouldn't have been physically able, no doubt
and any less, I would've chickened out
so, although my mind lost count,
my heart knew the perfect amount.

and if it wasn't for that bar, I wouldn't have found her
that's when I knew,
she was the one
I was right about that too

smile

my friends probably tell people that I "don't do much anymore"
they might say I'm lonely
sad or that I live my life in fear
but to be completely honest
it's quite the opposite
I haven't felt this good in years

on the surface though, they aren't wrong
I haven't been around in awhile
I value my privacy,
and battle some anxiety
but I like this life I live, quietly

I'm happy, finally

an athlete turned poet
I know, quite the difference & a little weird
but just like sports,
my stress while writing
just disappears

so, to my friends that might say "haven't seen him in a while"
I miss you guys
but I'm on mission to make the world smile

wipe it all away

in another universe
I'd get to watch
as your fingerprints
turn to wrinkles
your hand used to fit
so perfectly into mine

when will I start to forget?

I think that's the worst thing
about love...
it'd be a lot easier if we could just
wipe it all away once it's over

something real

what's with today's world of dating?
the one percent are serious and you told me that you are
but I've been over this before
you'll tell me you like me today but tomorrow
you'll find a new guy and be out the door

I hope you're different
& that you want something real
because I'm so over the girls who want no strings
attached and gauge their men
strictly off sex appeal

I'm not looking for "come over and watch a movie"
I want night drives, picnic dates
I want paint with pottery, the rink and roller skates
I want... the things that bring about real love

there are other guys that want this too
so, don't settle because your guy is out there
waiting for you

try to stop

(what I wanted to say vs. what I actually said)

~~before I left, two months ago, you told me to do this for myself. that you loved me but couldn't hold on while I went away. you had to go with your gut and decide not to stay.~~

~~it hurt but it was valid. how could you invest in eternity, with uncertainty?~~

~~I spent forty days and nights thinking about you. how I was getting better for you so that we can be together again. I filled my mind with memories to wash out my anxiety and depression. craving you kept me from craving nicotine. I'm sober now, but I need you. missing your laugh. being hypnotized by those eyes. longing for your lips. I know I haven't been perfect, but I've never been so sure that you are my future. because when I stood face to face with death, I remembered the life in yours. when can I see you?~~

~~let me prove that our promises are still our reality.~~

hey. I honestly still think about you every day but if you are trying to get over me then I will try to stop.

(it's been some time now. I've tried but I'll never be able to unlove you. hope you're doing well.)

special day

tomorrow's your special day
I learned as I overheard your conversation in the hallway
you'll turn twenty-one
I want to wish you a happy birthday, but that would be dumb

because I doubt you even know who I am
you're the girl in everyone's dream
the dream where you don't want to leave
the one that makes you believe
"I just found love in my sleep."

we have chem 101 together,
"today we assign new lab partners" claims the professor
he says my name "you'll be paired with ms. heather "
you sit down next to me,
my stomach in a blender

"how about this weather?" why would I say that
luckily you smile,
"it's nice" you say
class goes on, we laugh the whole time while doing our lab
as I'm packing up, you hit me with a little jab
you say, "we make a good team"
I agree

it's not a common theme
who would have thought
I'd land the girl in my dream?
that's a special day for me

lucky

you make life easier

one Sunday morning,
I woke up without my alarm going off
I took it as a warning
of a storm, forming

sleep is important to me
and usually my alarm keeps me in check
so that my days don't turn into a wreck

it took me a sec
for my phone to load and get moving
I had to see how you were doing

but you beat me to it
every letter, my day instantly better
your blue box says good morning with a wink
standing at my sink
I couldn't help to think

how

I'm so lucky to have you
you're a constant reminder
as long as my eyes can open
"I love you's" can be spoken
my heart will never be broken
because you're my golden token

so, put me on the news
I'd be able to prove that
in a crowd of millions,
you're the one I'd choose
because of that
I know I'll never lose

window shutters

behind her red, front door
a little, frail woman sits in her leather chair
in the house that occupies the top of my street
seeing her out of her home is rare
her smile as I drive by, a treat

she doesn't come outside often
which makes me wonder
how much of my life
she's seen behind her window shutters

did she see when I fell off my bike and busted my face?
did she watch when my friend and I would race?
did she witness my first kiss in the bus line?
did she notice my change in height when I turned nine?
did she ever want to fly that door open and come say hi?

what about the time I was on crutches
or the days I would go on a run
what about our summer lemonade stands
or the very noticeable burns I got from the sun

she's probably so lonely
there's never anyone coming or going
I should go knock on her door

because if I was the frail, old man
sitting in my leather chair
behind my red, front door
that's all I would ask for

a friend
that'll stay by my side
to the very end

my favorite introduction

check the clock, it's 2:41
pushing my cart, I look down the aisle
in total shock, your brown bun
and middle part, you hit me with that smile

angel on the right shoulder, devil on the other
heaven if I told you, hell I shouldn't even bother
I'll do it, tell you that your pretty, but no words come out
gone, the prettiest girl in the city like water in a drought

well, that's it, I thought
more fish in the sea, I was taught
but you were the fish I wish I'd caught
was excited for the time we'd tie the knot,
get a dog named spot,
cook our meals with our pot,
in our little cot,
then together wither and rot.

now it's only an afterthought
instead, I'm here standing in line
excited about the hot chicken I got

throwing my items on the belt, push my cart to the end
a tap on the back from the man behind me, a familiar friend

we get to talking and I had to tell him about you & why,
why I'd be the luckiest guy if I wasn't so shy and
had just stopped you to say
"hi, you shine like the brightest star in the sky."

"next time, I'll try." I say to him as I let out a sigh.
the brown bun, I notice you standing behind my friend in line
"how embarrassing", I thought. I think I want to die
screw it, I'll say something, at some point I got to try
I commit, open my mouth but before words come out
you say,

"I heard everything you said about me, I can tell you're a really sweet guy.
you could've saved those compliments for later because you would've had me at hi."

sometimes

to my future wife
I need to come clean
before we live and grow old together
there're a few things I need to tell you about
well, things about me

sometimes I can be a little too optimistic
when things get hard, I still want your life to be easy
I'm a glass half full type of guy, and a fan of the dad
jokes that are a little too cheesy

sometimes I can be a bit shy
when people boast and get loud, I tend to sit back and be quiet
because I've learned that most people take advantage
of the things you say
so now I keep most things private

sometimes I might need you a little more than you may need me
and I hope that's okay
because for some reason it's harder for me to find the light
when it's dark and world is gray

enough about me, I can't wait to learn everything
about you and how you live
when I can see you face to face, and not just in my dream
because the guy on the other side of your screen
wants you, your time, your love
and everything in between

1000

if a picture is worth 1000 words,
I hope my thousands of words paint pictures
that mend thousands of hearts

advantageous

everywhere you go, lighting up every room
but it's so subtle
like the night being lit up by the moon

the more you make other people smile
the easier it is for me to love you

your smile - famous
your love - contagious
and I get you on an everyday basis
advantageous

ebullience

ebullience (n.) - the quality of lively or enthusiastic expression of thoughts or feelings

a proud father describing the noble traits
of his wonderful daughter
an optimistic and thirsty wanderer praising mother
nature after finding a basin of water
an appreciative alum admiring the home-like
essence of her alma-mater

in this world where
war is normal,
power is desired,
and the focus is on self-destruction
instead of healing

since promises are forgotten...
and the answers,
have no intention of revealing

ebullient love is the resolution. it's exactly
what this world needs. love dealing.

addiction

I'm a year sober off of nicotine
$920 I would've had to pay
to make twelve months of pain go away
and I can honestly say

it got easier every day

getting over you has been a lot harder
and I think it's because
my addiction to you can't be valued by the dollar

but it's ok
life goes on and
I'll continue to pray

for the day
that the pain of losing you
decides it can't

stay

by Jalon Smith

from giving flowers to swiping right

left
left
left
left
                                        RIGHT- cute but short
left
                      RIGHT- gorgeous but lives too far away
left
left
left
            you skipped someone that likes you
left
left
left
                    RIGHT- wife material but dislikes sports
left
left
left
left
        RIGHT- smart and stunning but pictured with her name on an ashtray
left
left

what am I doing? what a shame...
I've caved into playing their stupid little game

love
you will find me, organically.
like running our shopping carts into each other at the store
helping you pick up the stuff that fell out of your car as you're struggling, frantically
or maybe sharing a cab with you on my first work trip in Baltimore

anyways, how many people on this app truly find the person that will make them complete?

see ya later

>   *delete "dating app"?*
> *deleting this app will also delete its data.*
>   **delete**

by Jalon Smith

hours

this girl commented on my video
and for some reason
I don't know,
I can't get her out of my head
she's following me everywhere I go

it's crazy

I saw her glittery eyes in the stars last night
her smile in the bubbles of my coffee
even the letters of her name protrude, as I write

her hair in my neighbors overgrown grass as it blows in the breeze
her teeth in the twitter picture of the houses
on the coast of Greece
I saw her figure in the shape of the glass vase
on my kitchen counter
and her beauty in the flowers
I wish I could ask her questions for hours

maybe if she comes around again
I might just let her know
until then I guess I'll just have to wait
and let the thought of her and I grow

I can't escape her
but do I even want to?

send me to hell

I've grown up loving God
I still do and always will
it's not even a question
but to be honest
I don't have an obsession to go to heaven

when I was seven, I drew a picture of myself in heaven so
I get it, it's not normal to think this way, I know
heaven is everyone's desired destination
before you judge and say I'm crazy
let me prove that I have a valid explanation

some might say I'm foolish for choosing to go anywhere else after death
and that a person with some sense probably wouldn't
but I don't really care to admit, I'd rather go somewhere
somewhere, that I probably shouldn't

you know, I'm not scared of hell
because I've already lived through it
back when the dark smothered the light
when life wasn't how I drew it
and when I all I wanted for life, was to redo it

back then I didn't care where I went
I just wanted to leave
but God kept me here for a reason
to wear my heart on my sleeve
and show others like me
that good things will come as long as you believe

I'm not gonna stop
and I don't want to when my life comes to an end
so, send me to hell
so I can give the hurt something to believe in

I'd love to see my loved ones up in heaven,
meet Jesus, the apostles, or other incredible people that have passed
can you do me a favor?
tell 'em I chose to spread love in hell
if they ask.

God put people in my life to pull me out of my hell on earth
I owe this to Him
for giving me purpose and showing me what I was worth

so, to answer your question...
why I no longer want the life after death
that was in the picture I drew when I was seven?

because I'd rather stay in hell just to make it someone's heaven

acknowledgements

God
Mom & Dad
Jackie & Elise
Brinkley
Jalon S & Lizzie K
Nio
Jermaine Cole & Zach Bryan
Lindner & Hopeway
Dr. JK
Dr. KS
Dr. KM
Dr. NF
Therapist DA
Life Coach GM
Altoids & Coffee

&
*the social media poetry community
that has taken me in.*

for my readers,
it's you who fueled this book.
until the next...
keep spreading love
-AN

shane a	meg r	madison c
nicole	ally	faith m
milana m	rachel k	josie g
keala f	adrianna	lydia z
saida f	lindsey	haley b
autumn l	celine g	rachel l
brianna m	kaitee	hampton r
maria v	cate	vic t
starlie b	izabella c	nimbus f
lindi s	hope b	tiffany d
erica d	hampton r	sofie w
seana	emma g	aaron o
sarah b	brittaney d	taylor s
betsy	michelle c	maria g
kamryne s	daniela l	rosen s
maddy a	jackie h	ayden w
kendra	renee	matina
christina	emerson m	paige r
alyson r	gracie m	neia p
hannah l	payton c	rosie z
marissa m	gaby r	becky g
berkley	craig n	kassandra b
reagan	carlie	britney w
cheyenne	jess k	nour z
carly	adrianna s	bharti b
rebekah c	dilan c	taylor r
ella n	ellen d	agrima b
clark d	lindsey b	ebony b
abby r	gina m	antwan w

gavin j	brianna e	jenna l
amara b	amelie s	ana d
michelle m	kj j	ana k
iqra t	cierra p	brooklyn s
samia l	alejandra r	john g
avina s	muyembe m	paulina m
emily m	ayleen l	matis c
karen f	matthew r	rachel r
matt u	jetta k	denzel g
melissa p	mireya d	raya n
katrina p	ruth k	maria o
isabella d	khushi p	valerie g
blair h	seth m	lyncy p
zamaris r	vibe j	elizabeth p
asees h	jane f	kiyomi r
kaleigh h	kajal d	aashvi s
gabriela f	katie p	jessie r
emalyn h	roos k	ayah g
lama k	gabriyelle h	leland h
paige g	mikayla w	tony m
mahdi a	kamalei h	lindsay u
anne j	daniella d	john e
jonah h	gabriella j	claize c
daniela s	julia k	bernice l
vishruta p	kris h	noemi b
shaurya t	kailey f	sam l
nancy h	alexis l	aleanndra e
grace s	vanessa f	martinez k
elizabeth a	journee s	monica p
abigail b	junior f	mary c
amrita s	emily o	yilin l
christina f	elmara a	jocelyn v
leilani s	taylor b	wiki s
maritza l	becca c	anushima k
jamia b	aisha s	aki'Lah m

about the author

Andrew Noelker, once a collegiate baseball player, is now pitching words and spreading positivity, peace and love in the most simple, humble way. Just one year ago, suffering in a world of anxiety and panic, Andrew was lost, searching for purpose. He has now found solace in his new field of writing, bravely showing the world an authentic and vulnerable side of himself.

You can find Andrew honing his skill at local coffee shops. Andrew currently resides in Hamilton, Ohio with his best canine, Brinkley.

Follow his social media pages to stay updated on what he has planned next!

TikTok: @poetrybyAN
Instagram: @andrewnoelker

Made in United States
North Haven, CT
01 August 2025